This book belongs to:

....

....

....

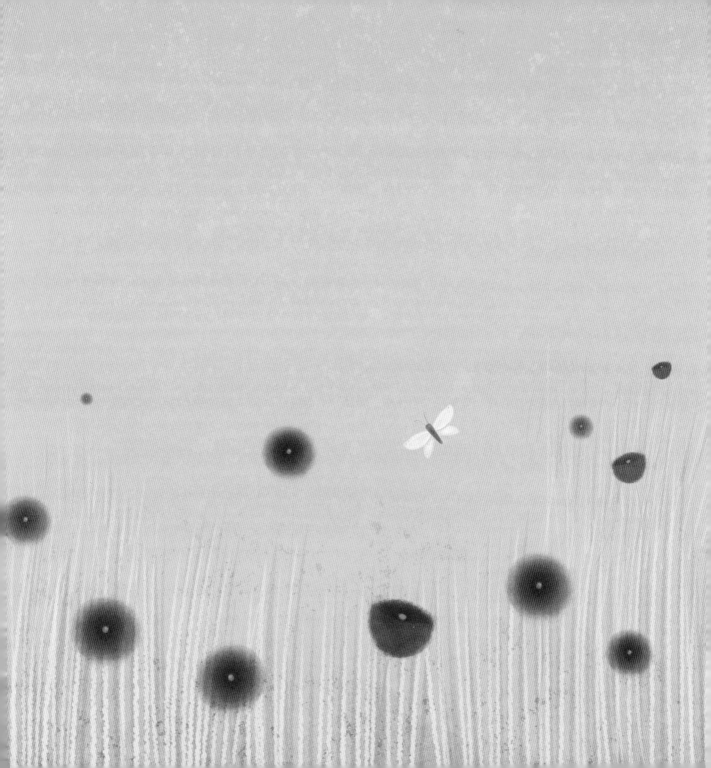

For C. T. x

tiger tales

5 River Road, Suite 128, Wilton, CT 06897
Published in the United States 2016
This collection copyright © 2016 Little Tiger Press
Illustrations copyright © 2016 Anna Jones
ISBN-13: 978-1-58925-486-2 • ISBN-10: 1-58925-486-4
Printed in China • LTP/1400/1450/0216

For more insight and activities, visit us at www.tigertalesbooks.com

My Little Book of

Bedtime
Prayers

Illustrated by
Anna Jones

tiger tales

Dear Father in Heaven

Dear Father in heaven,
Look down from above;
Bless Papa and Mama,
And those whom I love.

May angels guard over
My slumbers and when
The morning is breaking,
Awake me.

Amen.

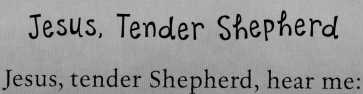

Jesus, Tender Shepherd

Jesus, tender Shepherd, hear me:
Bless Thy little child tonight;
Through the darkness be Thou near me,
Keep me safe 'til morning light.
All this day Thy hand has led me,
And I thank Thee for Thy care;

Thou hast warmed me, clothed me, fed me;
Listen to my evening prayer.
May my sins be all forgiven;
Bless the friends I love so well;
Watch me, Lord, as I am sleeping,
And guard me 'til the morning bell.

Thank You, God in Heaven

Thank you, God in heaven,
For sweet and simple joys—
Playtime shared with friends,
For laughter, games, and toys.

Thank you, God, for music,
And for all the songs we sing.
Our hearts are filled with happiness
With all the gifts You bring.

Watch Over a Little Child

Watch over a little child tonight,
Blessed Savior from above,
And keep me 'til the morning light
Within Your arms of love.

Amen.

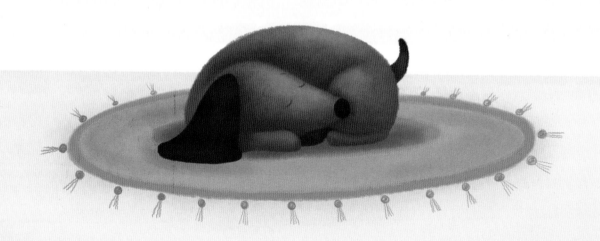

Now the Light Has Gone Away

Now the light has gone away;
Savior, listen while I pray.
Asking Thee to watch and keep
And to send me quiet sleep.
Jesus, Savior, wash away
All that has been wrong today;
Help me every day to be
Good and gentle, more like Thee.
Let my near and dear ones be
Always near and dear to Thee.

Matthew, Mark, Luke, and John

Matthew, Mark, Luke, and John,
Bless the bed that I lie on.
Four corners to my bed,
Four angels 'round my head.
One to watch and one to pray,
And two to guide me through the day.

The Lord's Prayer

Our Father, Who art in Heaven,
Hallowed be Thy name;
Thy kingdom come,
Thy will be done on Earth as it is in Heaven.
Give us this day our daily bread;
And forgive us our trespasses, as we forgive
those who trespass against us;
And lead us not into temptation,
But deliver us from evil.
For Thine is the kingdom, and the power,
and the glory forever and ever.

Amen.

Look Upon Thy Little Child

At the close of every day,
Lord, to Thee I kneel and pray.
Look upon Thy little child,
Look in love and mercy mild.
O forgive and wash away
All my naughtiness this day,
And both when I sleep and wake
Bless me for my Savior's sake.

The Day Is Done

The day is done;
O God the Son,
Look down upon
Thy little one!
O Light of Light,
Keep me this night,
And shed 'round me
Thy presence bright.
I need not fear
If Thou art near;
Thou art my Savior
Kind and dear.

Dear Heavenly Father

Dear Heavenly Father,
We thank You for our home.
It lives with You inside our hearts,
No matter where we roam.

You share all our sunny days,
And give shelter in the storm.
With Your love around us,
We'll be safe and sound and warm.

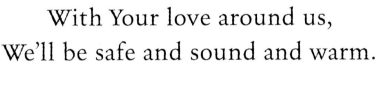

Now the Day Is Over

Now the day is over,
Night is drawing nigh,
Shadows of the evening
Steal across the sky.
Now the darkness gathers,
Stars begin to peep,
Birds and beasts and flowers
Soon will be asleep.

All Through the Night

Sleep, my child, and peace attend thee,
All through the night.
Guardian angels God will send thee,
All through the night.

Soft the drowsy hours are creeping,
Hill and vale in slumber steeping,
I my loving vigil keeping,
All through the night.